December 25, 2015

Merry Christmas, Wilfred!

Nana and Grandpa look
forward to seeing
Cincinnati with you!

HARRIETT'S HOMECOMING

A High-Flying Tour of Cincinnati

SUSAN SACHS LEVINE

Illustrated by Erin Burchwell

ORANGE *frazer* PRESS

Wilmington, Ohio

ISBN 978-1933197-975

Additional copies of *Harriett's Homecoming: A High-Flying Tour of Cincinnati* may be ordered directly from:
Orange Frazer Press
P.O. Box 214
Wilmington, OH 45177
Telephone 1.800.852.9332 for price and shipping information.
Website: www.orangefrazer.com

Watercolor paints were used for the full color art.
Book and cover design: Brittany Lament and Orange Frazer Press

Factbox photos by and courtesy of Susan Sachs Levine and Erin Burchwell unless otherwise noted: page 6 courtesy of Robert Webber; page 9, top photo courtesy of Cincinnati Parks; page 9, bottom photo courtesy of Cincinnati Arts Association; page 10 courtesy of Martin Milligan; page 11 courtesy of Public Library of Cincinnati; page 13 courtesy of Dave Jenike; page 15 courtesy of University of Cincinnati; page 17, photo on left courtesy of Cincinnati Parks; page 17, photo on right courtesy of Tony Arrasmith & Associates; page 18, top photo courtesy of Gary Kessler; page 18, bottom photo courtesy of Cincinnati Art Museum; page 21 courtesy of Newport Aquarium; page 22 courtesy of National Underground Railroad Freedom Center; page 24, top photo courtesy of Cincinnati Parks; page 24, bottom photo courtesy of 3CDC (Cincinnati Center City Development Corp); page 27, left photo courtesy of Tony Ravagnani; page 27, right photo courtesy of Kings Island.

Susan Levine would like to thank Mykl Sandusky, docent at the Cincinnati Museum Center, for his assistance with historical facts about Cincinnati. She would also like to thank her friend Ellie Jeffers for being a great editor.

Library of Congress Control Number: 2012943725
First printing, 2012

July, 2012
Printed by Everbest Printing Co., Ltd., Guangdong, China
Job Batch #107223

To my family, for all their love, support and laughs. —Susan Sachs Levine

For Gracie Jane and all the wonderful people who played with her while I worked on this book. —Erin Burchwell

High up on the rooftop of the Carew Tower in downtown Cincinnati, a young peregrine falcon timidly lifts off from a wildlife officer's hand.

"Go on, Harriett, head for home," coaxes the officer.

It has been ten days since Harriett crashed into the window of a skyscraper while learning to fly. Rescued from the street below, Harriett was nursed back to health at a wildlife rehabilitation center.

The Carew Tower, in the heart of downtown, has graced the Cincinnati skyline for over eighty years and is designated a National Historic Landmark. Completed in 1930, it stands forty nine stories tall and is comprised of 4,000,000 bricks, 8,000 windows, and 5,000 doors. With impressive art deco architecture, the Carew Tower was used as a model for the Empire State Building in New York City. A rooftop observation deck is open to the public and offers spectacular views of the city.

The John A. Roebling Suspension Bridge spans the Ohio River between Cincinnati and Covington, Kentucky, and is on the National Register of Historic Places. Designed by John A. Roebling, work began in 1856 but the bridge was not completed until a decade later due to the Civil War. When opened in 1867, it was the longest suspension bridge in the world at 1,057 feet and one million pounds of cable. A toll of 15 cents was charged for a horse and buggy and pedestrians paid a penny. John Roebling went on to design the Brooklyn Bridge which was completed in 1883.

If I can just get to Fountain Square, where Mom and Dad taught me to hunt, thought Harriett, *I'll be able to find my nest.*

Gaining confidence, Harriett glided over the river and past a beautiful, blue, open-air castle that was suspended over the river like magic. Then she noticed several black tracks all going in the same direction. *Maybe those lead to Fountain Square*, observed Harriett.

Cincinnati Museum Center is located in Union Terminal just northwest of downtown. Built in 1933 for freight and passenger train service, Union Terminal is a National Historic Landmark and known for its magnificent art deco architecture. The popularity of cars and planes resulted in its closure in the early 1970s. Today, Union Terminal houses three separate museums and an Omnimax theater. The Cincinnati History Museum features a ninety-four-foot side-wheel steamboat called the "Queen of the West," that you can board. A huge mastodon skeleton greets you at the entrance of the Museum of Natural History. The Duke Energy Children's Museum has The Woods exhibit where you can climb, crawl and explore.

Cincinnati is often referred to as the Queen City. This can be traced back to the 1920s after Cincinnati experienced spectacular growth and was, according to its proud citizens, the "Queen of the West."

The tracks ended at a huge semi-circle building. Harriett flared her tail and landed at the edge of a magnificent, green, scalloped fountain. A handsome cat greeted her with a nod.

"Is this Fountain Square, sir?" asked Harriett, trying to be polite.

"Of course not," replied the cat. "This is the Cincinnati Museum Center, home to the Queen of the West. I'm the captain, and I grant you purrrrr-mission to board. I've got her docked just inside."

"Wow, I'd love to meet a real queen!" exclaimed Harriett.

Inside, a monster with big tusks and no skin glared at her.

Suddenly, Harriett was sucked down into a huge forest on silver moving steps. "Yikes!" she screeched.

There were children everywhere climbing, crawling, and disappearing into some trees and popping out of others. Turning around, Harriett came face-to-face with a little girl in a net cage.

I've had enough of cages at the wildlife center, thought Harriett. *I'm out of here. I'll meet the queen another day.*

Out the door and into the safety of the sky, Harriett headed north. Some music and a fountain soon caught her attention, and she swooped down to investigate.

A stream of water shot up as the music boomed and nearly knocked Harriett over. Just as suddenly, the water disappeared and shot up a few feet away. Then it disappeared and re-appeared again.

"Hey, who's playing a trick on me? I just want to find Fountain Square!" exclaimed a confused Harriett.

"Trick? Trick! I know tricks—sit, shake, even roll-over," piped up a puppy. "My friends probably know more, too." With a quick bark, a pack of dogs started running toward Harriett. She rose swiftly up into the sky just as they reached her.

Located just north of downtown in the historic Over-the-Rhine, Washington Park has recently undergone a total renovation. You can enjoy an open-air performance stage, a Cincinnati-themed playground, a dog park, and a state-of-the-art water plaza with more than 130 pop-up jets, which are synchronized to music and lights.

Cincinnati Music Hall is located directly across from Washington Park and serves as a magnificent backdrop. Built in 1878, in a Victorian Gothic style, it houses one of the nation's most beautiful concert halls. Known for its excellent acoustics, Music Hall is home to the Cincinnati Symphony/Pops Orchestras, the Cincinnati Opera, the Cincinnati Ballet and the May Festival Chorus.

Findlay Market is located in Over-the-Rhine, a neighborhood that was popular with German immigrants because it reminded them of the Rhine River Valley in Germany. Findlay Market was founded in 1852 and is the oldest public market in Ohio. Today the market area is easily recognized by its colorful "checkerboard" of awnings and flower boxes. Three dozen permanent merchants sell meat, fish, spices, produce, and cheeses. Special events at the market include the Opening Day Parade that marks the start of baseball season and the oldest German Day celebration in the U.S. complete with an "oom pah" band.

Nearby, Harriett noticed a colorful checkerboard below and dove down to check it out. People were bustling around buying fruits, vegetables, flowers, meats, and spices.

Maybe they have quail, she thought hopefully, remembering her favorite meal at the wildlife center.

A band on the square began playing a catchy tune—"oom pah pah, oom pah pah." Harriett started tapping her talons to the beat, but then suddenly felt sad. The song reminded her of her father, Papa. "I must find my home!" she said with determination, and took off.

What looked to be a fountain came into view. "Oh pleeeease let this be Fountain Square," Harriett pleaded.

When she landed, however, Harriett discovered that the sidewalk had sprung a leak and some books were getting wet! She tried to lift one up and drag it to safety, but it was too heavy.

She spotted a pig nearby pulling a cart. "Excuse me, but can you help me save the books from the flood?" asked Harriett.

"There's no flood, silly. That was 1937. Besides, my wagon is full," replied the pig.

Discouraged that she could not help, Harriett set off once more.

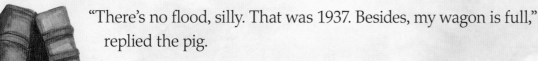

The Cincinnati Main Library has a unique "book fountain" out front, which was designed by Cincinnati sculptor Michael Frasca. The library opened in 1853 and was among the first libraries in America. In the Children's Learning Center Garden, you can see three sculptures including a mixed media "pig" that was designed to celebrate Cincinnati's pork packing heritage. Don't miss the Cincinnati panorama photograph that was taken in 1848 and is on display in the library. This eight plate image shows two miles of the historic Cincinnati riverfront.

January 1937 remains the wettest month ever recorded in Ohio and resulted in the worst flooding in Cincinnati's history. The Ohio River crested at nearly eighty feet and many parts of the city were underwater for nineteen days. The city's water supply was lost, streetcar service was curtailed and gas tanks exploded, resulting in great fires.

Harriett was searching the ground below when another fountain came into view. "Hooray!" she shouted. "This just HAS to be Fountain Square."

Descending for a near perfect landing, Harriett found herself staring at a beautiful blue bird in an intricate lace dress. "Are you the princess of Fountain Square?" inquired Harriett.

"This isn't Fountain Square," replied the bird. "It's the Cincinnati Zoo. By the way, I'm a boy!"

Oops, odd outfit, thought Harriett. Looking around she saw more unusual creatures. Some had necks so long their heads were lost in the clouds. Another had a nose so long it dragged on the ground! Suddenly, the gray creature lifted its nose and let out an earth-shaking trumpet. Harriett escaped to the sky.

Remembering that it's best to fly up high to spot prey, Harriett headed up a nearby hill thinking the same might be true for spotting fountains.

The Cincinnati Zoo & Botanical Garden opened in 1875, making it the second oldest zoo in the nation. It was named a National Historic Landmark in 1987 due to the interesting architecture of some of its original buildings such as the Reptile House, which is the oldest existing zoo building in the country. The Cincinnati Zoo has a long history of successful breeding programs, starting in 1878 when the first sea lion was born in captivity. During the summer months, you can enjoy giraffe feedings, elephant baths, and cheetahs racing at top speed.

Legend has it that Cincinnati is built on seven hills, just like Rome. The problem is that no one seems to be able to agree on the seven. While many lists disagree, all seem to have two hills in common—Mt. Adams and Mt. Auburn. Today, Mt. Adams is a residential area with winding streets, unique shops, and spectacular views. Mt. Auburn is known for its houses from the turn of the century when prominent citizens moved there to escape the dirt, smoke, and crowds of the city.

Looking down, Harriett saw two fierce lions guarding a tower. Several baby ducks were riding a log flume nearby.

Now there is a snack I can sink my beak into, thought Harriett, but when she caught one in her talons, it was rubbery on the outside and empty on the inside. "No lunch here!" exclaimed Harriett. "No Fountain Square either," she added sadly.

"SSSSSSSSSSSSSSay there little bird, you looking for a fountain?" hissed a snake. "Come over to my houssssse. We have a fountain."

Oh, what's the harm? thought Harriett, as she fell into step behind the slithering little "gardener" snake.

A hopeful Harriett followed the snake inside a building with a sign that read William Howard Taft Visitor Center and then burst out laughing at the "fountain" he proudly pointed toward.

"Thanks for your help little guy, but that's not exactly what I'm looking for."

"Maybe in the housssssse," offered the snake, starting up the hill.

"A time portal to the past!" Harriett proclaimed, upon entering. The furniture, books, portraits, toys, and piano were all really old and beautiful.

Then without warning a white head appeared in the corner, and Harriett backed quickly out the door. "Ghost!" she screamed as she catapulted herself into the sky.

The University of Cincinnati was founded in 1819 and today has over 42,000 students. The largest college on campus is the College of Arts and Sciences located in McMicken Hall. Two stone lions, named Mick and Mack, adorn the entrance of McMicken Hall and have become symbols of the University. "Duck races," in the nearby fountain, mark the arrival of spring each year.

The William Howard Taft National Historic Site was established in 1969 in the house where the former President and Chief Justice of the Supreme Court was raised. Located in Mt. Auburn, the two-story Greek Revival house has been restored to 1857 when William was born. A bust of his father, Alphonso, resides in the parlor. The original white marble bust can be seen at the Taft Museum of Art. Taft was the first president to preside over forty-eight states, when New Mexico and Arizona were added in 1912. He was also the first president to own a car at the White House. Be sure to look for the garter snakes that park rangers report nest in the stone wall next to the house!

15

With a couple flaps of her powerful wings, Harriett was aloft and headed up the next hill. Sure enough, a fountain came into view. "Oh please be Fountain Square!" she begged.

Several squirrels were hiking by when she landed. "Is this Fountain Square?" Harriett inquired.

"No, Miss. Scouts' honor," replied the head squirrel. "This is Eden Park. The boys are just finishing up their tree identification badge. Got to know where to find acorns come fall."

16

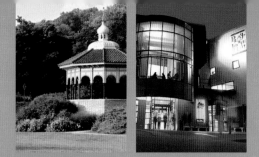

Just five minutes from downtown in Mt. Adams, Eden Park truly is Cincinnati's Garden of Eden. It is over 180 acres and features several lakes, historic structures, and gardens. Best known are Mirror Lake, the Bettman Fountain, the Spring House Gazebo, Elsinore Tower, and the Presidential Tree Grove. In Eden Park you can also visit the Cincinnati Art Museum, Cincinnati Playhouse in the Park, and the Krohn Conservatory.

The Cincinnati Playhouse in the Park is nestled on a hillside in the heart of Eden Park. Started in 1959, the Playhouse is one of America's first regional theatres. Today it offers productions ten months out of the year in two theatres. The Playhouse is committed to producing a variety of classic, contemporary, and world premiere works. A Saturday performance series for children, touring shows, and acting classes are a few ways you can experience the Playhouse for yourself.

Looking around, Harriett watched families playing and enjoying picnics. Then she saw something that alarmed her. A boy had a beautiful, big bird on a string. The bird struggled to get free, but the boy held tight. *I had better get out of here before they tie me up*, thought Harriett.

The Krohn Conservatory opened in 1933 and will celebrate its 80th anniversary in 2013. It was constructed in the art deco style as reflected in the beautiful window etchings, terrazzo entry floor, and hand rails. The rock used in the beds is locally quarried dolomitic limestone. The Conservatory is divided into five different houses including the Palm House which features a twenty-foot waterfall and the Desert House which has a variety of cacti.

The Cincinnati Art Museum was heralded worldwide as the "Art Palace of the West" when it opened in 1886 in Cincinnati's Eden Park. Today the permanent collection includes more than 60,000 works spanning 6,000 years. The Museum reaches out to families by hosting Family First Saturdays each month that feature performers, scavenger hunts, and hands-on art.

A stream of water inside a glass building caught her attention. Harriett banked right and glided down. A ladybug was collecting greens nearby. "Is this Fountain Square?" asked Harriett.

"Non, non. Voilà, le Krohn Conservatory! It's almost time for le dîner. Today I am preparing a delicious salade verte. Bon appétit!" announced the ladybug, dramatically.

"A bowl of green leaves? Not exactly my idea of a good meal," remarked Harriett.

Heading inside, Harriett found a jungle of salad fixins—giant ferns, flowers, and trees. A huge waterfall splashed water and Harriett enjoyed a much deserved drink.

Now I just need a quick rest on these plant pillows, she thought, but when she sat down, a thousand pins pricked her behind. She shot up like a rocket and was out the door.

Bon appétit!

19

Back in the sky, Harriett headed across the river. She spotted a fountain and a big bird in a tuxedo. "Is this Fountain Square?" asked Harriett, feeling a bit under-dressed.

"Why no, young lady. This is the Newport Aquarium. Allow me," replied the bird with a bow, as he opened the door.

Inside, Harriett was enchanted by a room filled with little dancing umbrellas. Suddenly, she realized they were all underwater. "The flood is coming!" she exclaimed. Harriett turned to run and found herself surrounded by more water. It was filled with fish, turtles, eels, and coral, but she was not getting wet. There was an invisible wall holding back the water!

The Newport Aquarium, located on the Levee, showcases thousands of animals from around the world including the rarely seen shark ray. Don't miss the Penguin Parade that opens the Aquarium each morning. You will also enjoy the Jellyfish Gallery which features hundreds of these graceful creatures and the eighty-five-foot shark tunnel where you can watch several species swim peacefully overhead. Nearby, at the Shark Central exhibit, you can even touch a shark.

Newport on the Levee is an entertainment area located on the Ohio River in Newport, Kentucky. It can be easily reached by car or a walk across the "Purple People Bridge." Restaurants, shops, a movie theatre, a bowling alley, and an aquarium are just some of the attractions. To experience the Ohio River, you can Ride the Ducks, which are amphibious tour vehicles that leave directly from the Levee. At nearby BB Riverboats, you can take a cruise aboard a paddle wheeler.

Just then, a huge creature sporting rows and rows of fierce-looking teeth swam by. *Must be friends with the tooth fairy,* observed Harriett. *Don't think I'll stick around to ask. Time to find home.*

The National Underground Railroad Freedom Center, located near the riverfront in Cincinnati, tells the story of slavery in the Americas, from its introduction to its abolition at the end of the American Civil War. The events are portrayed through exhibits, movies, and interactive displays. Highlights include an original 170-year-old slave pen where men, women, and children were kept before they were "auctioned off," and a beautiful tapestry by famed folk artist Aminah Robinson.

Cincinnati prides itself on its professional sports teams, the five-time World Series Champion Cincinnati Reds and the two-time Super Bowl runners-up, Cincinnati Bengals. The Cincinnati Red Stockings were baseball's first professional franchise in 1869. The Great American Ballpark is home to the Reds. Its design recalls the history of Cincinnati and includes a "Riverboat Deck" with tall stacks that shoot fireworks every time the Reds hit a home run. The Bengals were founded in 1967 by football Hall of Famer, Paul Brown. You can see a game in the Bengals' new stadium which is named in his honor.

Down by the river, Harriett met a muskrat. "Looking to cross the river to freedom?" asked the muskrat, elated to have a traveler after all these years.

"I'm actually looking for Fountain Square," replied Harriett.

"Be very quiet and follow me," instructed the muskrat, as he started across.

On the opposite bank was a big building. Peering in, Harriett saw a huge, colorful tapestry on the wall and an old wooden building. *A building inside a building, that's weird*, she thought.

Kaboom! Kaboom! Fire started spitting out of the top of two big towers next door, frightening Harriett.

"No worries, just a home run," assured the muskrat.

"Run home! That's what I want to do," said Harriett, excitedly.

"Well then, go my friend, straight north. Don't let them tag you out," cried the muskrat.

23

Extending from the Great American Ballpark to Paul Brown Stadium is the newest riverfront feature in Cincinnati, Smale Riverfront Park. This recreational center has water jets and cascades, a glass-floored walkway, a stage and event lawn, a tree grove, gardens, and a labyrinth.

The Tyler Davidson Fountain, the focal point on Fountain Square, was presented to the people of Cincinnati in 1871 by Henry Probasco. The bronze fountain glorifies water. The central figure at the top represents the Genius of Water. From her outstretched arms, water flows down past sculptures that represent the practical uses of water, such as watering crops. The sculptures of children at the edge show the pleasures of water. The fountain has become one of Cincinnati's best known and most beloved symbols.

Harriett started to run up the street, in the direction the muskrat had pointed, faster than she'd ever run in her life. "Whoa, ouch, don't step on me," screamed Harriett as she weaved through the people. "I just want to go home."

Out of breath, Harriett staggered into a big square.
To her delight, she heard a familiar voice.

"Harriett, is that you?"

She looked up, and there, perched on the top of a big fountain,
was her sister, Maria. "We've been so worried about you,"
she stammered. "Where have you been?"

"Maria!" cried Harriett, bobbing her head up and down.
"Let's go home!"

"Did you find lunch, Maria?" her mother asked.

"Something better than lunch, Mom," replied Maria.

Harriett swooped in and they both yelled, "Surprise!"

Oh, how they all celebrated Harriett's homecoming—whistling, circling until they were dizzy.

"Tomorrow, let's take the day off and have some fun seeing all the sites around Cincinnati," suggested Harriett's father. "I know a great aquarium and a zoo and…"

26

The Fourth and Vine Tower is easily recognized by its unique square top. Completed in 1913, the building was the fifth tallest in the world and the tallest in Cincinnati. It lost that distinction when the Carew Tower was completed in 1930. Today, the Fourth and Vine Tower houses financial, law, and insurance companies. (And, of course, a family of peregrine falcons!)

Kings Island is an amusement and water park located twenty miles north of Cincinnati. It offers over eighty rides, shows and attractions including fourteen roller coasters and a fifteen acre Soak City water park. At Kings Island you can experience the 80 mph Diamondback roller coaster and The Beast, the longest wooden roller coaster in the world.

But Harriett wasn't listening; she was so happy to be home that she had fallen asleep and was already dreaming about her next big adventure.

Author's Note

Peregrine falcons were first introduced into downtown Cincinnati in 1990 as part of the Peregrine Falcon Restoration Project. Other cities in Ohio such as Columbus, Akron, and Dayton participated as well, releasing juvenile falcons each spring until 1992. The falcons were banded so that they could be tracked and monitored. Peregrine falcon numbers had plummeted in the 1960s due to the use of pesticides like DDT. The 27th floor of the Fourth and Vine Tower was selected as the site to build a nesting platform because the skyscraper could simulate the high cliffs that the peregrines prefer.

In 1993, Cincinnati had its first successful nest at Fourth and Vine. The female was a falcon that had been released in Pictured Rocks, Michigan, as part of the recovery program, while the male, Falcor, had been released in Cincinnati. Together they produced just four chicks from 1993 to 1999, with several failed nesting attempts.

In the spring of 2000, Falcor teamed up with a new female named Princess, who hatched in Wisconsin two years earlier. Over the next three years, Falcor and Princess successfully fledged seven young. In 2003, Falcor must have encountered some difficulty as he disappeared from the area and there was no nesting attempt. Luckily, Princess stayed in the area, found a new mate, and has successfully raised chicks every year since. In fact, she has added 28 young to her "chick count" since 2004. Most recently, two males named Skyline and Red Legs were hatched and banded in the spring of 2012. With a success record like that, she truly is the "princess" of the Queen City!

In 2010, while learning to fly, one of Princess' young, a female named Flo, crashed into the window of a nearby skyscraper and fell to the street below. It is not unusual for the young birds to have encounters with glass as it is hard for them to see. Rescued by concerned citizens, Flo was taken to RAPTOR, Inc., a rehabilitation center for birds of prey. There she was nursed back to health on a diet primarily of quail. After demonstrating that she could fly and bank for turns in a large flight cage, Flo was taken to the observation deck of the Carew Tower and released. She made it back to the Fourth and Vine Tower, where she was successfully reunited with her family and became the inspiration for Harriett's story.

In Cincinnati, the ODNR Division of Wildlife monitors the falcon nest at the Fourth and Vine Tower. To see a peregrine falcon up close and learn more about how they are rehabilitated, contact RAPTOR, Inc. at www.raptorinc.org or call 513-825-3325.

Princess feeding her chicks.

Photo by Sister Marty Dermody

29

Learn More About Peregrine Falcons

The peregrine falcon, historically known as the "Duck Hawk," is a large raptor about the size of a crow. Its habitat ranges all the way from the Arctic Tundra to the Tropics, making it the world's most widespread falcon. The adult peregrine is a handsome bird with a blue-gray back and head, and a "mustache." The under parts are barred white. As with other birds of prey, the female is significantly bigger than the male.

Peregrine falcons return to the same nesting spot year after year. They do not bring any materials to build a nest, they simply make a depression in the dirt or gravel of the nesting ledge. In North America, mating behavior can usually be seen beginning in late January and February, and by March or April three to four eggs will be laid. The eggs are slightly smaller than a chicken egg.

The male and female take turns incubating the eggs. When the chicks hatch, they are covered in a creamy-white down. The chicks fledge, or learn to fly, about 45 days after hatching, replacing their white fluff with the sleek brown flying feathers of a juvenile. They remain dependent on their parents for food for as long as two months.

Peregrine falcons hunt during daylight hours, feeding primarily on birds ranging in size from a sparrow to a duck. Once the peregrine spots its prey, it can dive at speeds over 200 mph, making it the fastest animal on our planet! As the peregrine closes in on prey, it balls up its feet and strikes the prey, killing it. The peregrine then swoops down, grabbing the prey with its talons and returns to the nest. In urban areas, feral pigeons are a common prey along with starlings, mourning doves, and even songbirds. The male does the majority of the hunting for the female and young chicks. The adults will generally pluck the feathers from the prey for the young before they eat.

Peregrine falcons keep the same mate from year to year, but if one of the pair is injured or killed, the other will quickly seek a new mate. On average, peregrines have a lengthy lifespan of 12-15 years in the wild. Due to successful breeding and introduction programs, peregrine falcons were removed from the Federal Endangered Species List in 1999. The species was down-listed to "threatened" in Ohio in 2009.

Why Harriett?

When picking a name for the main character in my book, I wanted a connection to Cincinnati. I chose Harriett to honor Harriet Beecher Stowe, abolitionist and author of *Uncle Tom's Cabin*. She met her husband and had six of her seven children in Cincinnati. The Stowes supported the Underground Railroad and housed fugitives in their home. *Uncle Tom's Cabin*, published in 1852, revealed the harsh realities of slavery to the world and energized anti-slavery forces in the American north.

Harriett's sister, Maria, is named after Maria Longworth Nichols Storer. A lover of the arts and talented ceramic painter, Maria founded Rookwood Pottery in 1880 and was one of the first women in Cincinnati to own a large business. Rookwood Pottery went on to become world famous.

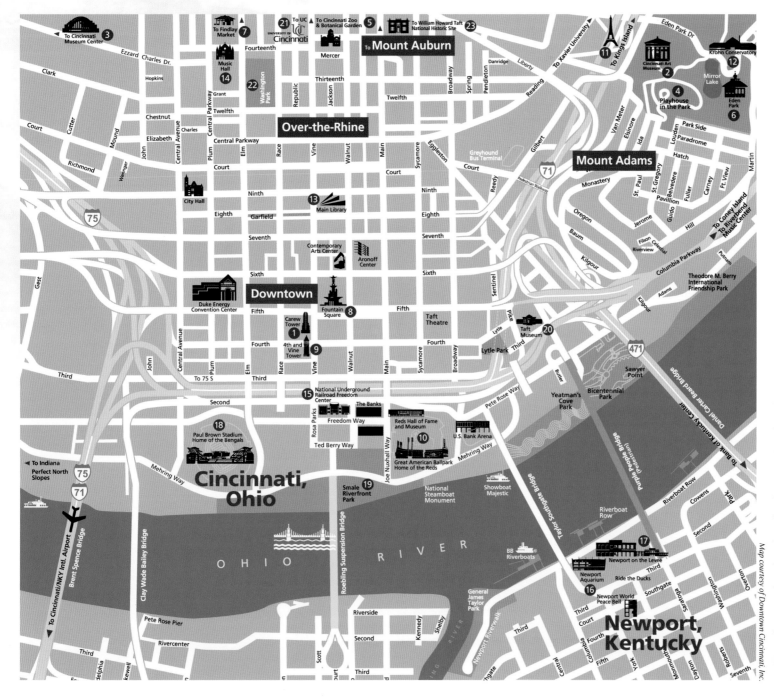

To Cincinnati Museum Center ▶

3

To Findlay Market

7

UNIVERSITY OF Cincinnati

To UC

21

To Cincinnati Zoo & Botanical Garden

5

To William Howard Taft National Historic Site

23

Mount Auburn

To Xavier University

11

To Kings Island

Cincinnati Art Museum

2

Krohn Conservatory

12

Ezzard Charles Dr.

Clark

Hopkins

Chestnut

Elizabeth

Richmond

Court

Fourteenth

Mercer

Thirteenth

Twelfth

Music Hall

14

Grant

Twelfth

Charles

22

Washington Park

Central Parkway

Court

Eden Park Dr

Mirror Lake

4

Playhouse in the Park

Eden Park

6

Danridge

Liberty

Broadway

Spring

Pendleton

Reading

Gilbert

Van Meter

Elsinore

Ida

Louden

Park Side

Paradrome

Hatch

Over-the-Rhine

Central Avenue

Central Parkway

Clark

Cutter

Mound

John

Wenger

Court

Plum

Central Parkway

Elm

Race

Vine

Walnut

Main

Sycamore

Eggleston

Court

Greyhound Bus Terminal

71

Pedestrian Walkway

Reedy

Sentinel

Mount Adams

Monastery

St. Paul

St. Gregory

Belvedere

Guido

Pavillion

Fuller

Carney

Ft. View

Martin

City Hall

75

Ninth

Eighth

Garfield

Seventh

Sixth

Ninth

Eighth

Seventh

Sixth

Oregon

Jerome

Baum

Kilgour

Filson

Riverview

Celestial

Columbia Parkway

To Coney Island To Riverbend Music Center ▶

Main Library

13

Contemporary Arts Center

Aronoff Center

Theodore M. Berry International Friendship Park

Adams

Kilgour

Putnam

Duke Energy Convention Center

Downtown

Fifth

Fourth

Fountain Square

8

Fifth

Taft Theatre

Taft Museum

20

Pike

Lytle

Lytle Park

Third

471

Sawyer Point

Daniel Carter Beard Bridge

Carew Tower

1

4th and Vine Tower

9

Third

To 75 S

Fourth

Walnut

Main

Sycamore

Broadway

Butler

Third

Bicentennial Park

Yeatman's Cove Park

National Underground Railroad Freedom Center

15

Second

Rosa Parks

The Banks

Freedom Way

Ted Berry Way

Pete Rose Way

Paul Brown Stadium Home of the Bengals

18

Reds Hall of Fame and Museum

U.S. Bank Arena

Purple People Bridge (pedestrian)

To Bank of Kentucky Center ▶

◀ To Indiana Perfect North Slopes

75

71

Mehring Way

Great American Ballpark Home of the Reds

10

Joe Nuxhall Way

Mehring Way

Cincinnati, Ohio

◀ To Cincinnati/NKY Intl. Airport

Brent Spence Bridge

Clay Wade Bailey Bridge

Pete Rose Pier

Rivercenter

Third

Smale Riverfront Park

19

Roebling Suspension Bridge

National Steamboat Monument

Showboat Majestic

Riverboat Row

Cowens

Park

Second

BB Riverboats

Taylor Southgate Bridge

Riverboat Row

Newport on the Levee

17

Third

Second

Overton

Washington

Saratoga

O H I O   R I V E R

Newport Aquarium

Ride the Ducks

16

Newport World Peace Bell

Newport, Kentucky

General James Taylor Park

Newport Riverwalk

Riverside

Second

Kennedy

Shelby

Third

Court

Third

Fifth

York

Dayton

Roberts

Seventh

Map courtesy of Downtown Cincinnati, Inc.

You may wish to visit many of the wonderful sites mentioned in this book. To help plan your tour, use this map and the contact information on the following page. Enjoy!

1. **Carew Tower**
441 Vine Street
Cincinnati, Ohio 45202
513-241-3888

2. **Cincinnati Art Museum**
953 Eden Park Drive
Cincinnati, Ohio 45202
513-721-2787
www.cincinnatiartmuseum.org

3. **Cincinnati Museum Center**
1301 Western Avenue
Cincinnati, Ohio 45203
1-800-733-2077
www.cincymuseum.org

4. **Cincinnati Playhouse in the Park**
962 Mount Adams Circle
Cincinnati, Ohio 45202
513-421-3888
www.cincyplay.com

5. **Cincinnati Zoo & Botanical Garden**
3400 Vine Street
Cincinnati, Ohio 45220
513-281-4700
www.cincinnatizoo.org

6. **Eden Park**
950 Eden Park Drive
Cincinnati, Ohio 45202
513-352-4080
www.cincinnatiparks.com

7. **Findlay Market**
1801 Race Street
Cincinnati, Ohio 45202
513-665-4839
www.findlaymarket.org

8. **Fountain Square**
520 Vine Street
Cincinnati, Ohio 45202
513-763-8036
www.myfountainsquare.com

9. **Fourth and Vine Tower**
1 West Fourth Street
Cincinnati, Ohio 45202
513-621-4090

10. **Great American Ball Park and Reds Hall of Fame**
100 Joe Nuxhall Way
Cincinnati, Ohio 45202
For tickets call 513-381-REDS
www.cincinnati.reds.mlb.com

11. **Kings Island**
6300 Kings Island Drive
Mason, Ohio 45040
513-754-5700
www.visitkingsisland.com

12. **Krohn Conservatory**
1501 Eden Park Drive
Cincinnati, Ohio 45202
513-421-5707
www.cincinnatiparks.com

13. **Main Library of the Public Library of Cincinnati and Hamilton County**
800 Vine Street
Cincinnati, Ohio 45202
513-369-6900
www.cincinnatilibrary.org/main

14. **Music Hall, Cincinnati Symphony/ Pops, Cincinnati Opera, Cincinnati Ballet, May Festival Chorus**
1241 Elm Street
Cincinnati, Ohio 45202
513-744-3344, or for tickets 513-381-3300
www.cincinnatiarts.org/musichall

15. **National Underground Railroad Freedom Center**
50 East Freedom Way
Cincinnati, Ohio 45202
513-333-7500
www.freedomcenter.org

16. **Newport Aquarium**
1 Aquarium Way
Newport, Kentucky 41071
859-261-7444
www.newportaquarium.com

17. **Newport on the Levee**
1 Levee Way
Newport, Kentucky 41071
1-866-LEVEEKY
www.newportonthelevee.com

18. **Paul Brown Stadium**
One Paul Brown Stadium
Cincinnati, Ohio 45202
For tickets 513-621-8383
www.bengals.com

19. **Smale Riverfront Park**
Intersection of Mehring Way
and Joe Nuxhall Way
Cincinnati, Ohio 45202
513-352-4080
www.cincinnatiparks.com

20. **Taft Art Museum**
316 Pike Street
Cincinnati, Ohio 45202
513-241-0343
www.taftmuseum.org

21. **University of Cincinnati**
2600 Clifton Avenue
Cincinnati, Ohio 45221
513-556-6000
www.uc.edu

22. **Washington Park**
Elm Street between 12th and 14th Streets
Cincinnati, Ohio 45202
513-352-4080
www.cincinnatiparks.com

23. **William Howard Taft National Historic Site**
2038 Auburn Avenue
Cincinnati, Ohio 45219
513-684-3262
www.nps.gov/wiho